Songs of Papa's Island

Barbara Kerley

Illustrated by Katherine Tillotson

Houghton Mifflin Company
Boston   1995

For Scott and Anna:
Yahooey!

— B.K.

Library of Congress Cataloging-in-Publication Data

Kerley, Barbara.
   Songs of Papa's island / by Barbara Kerley ; illustrated by
Katherine Tillotson.
      p.   cm.
   Summary: A mother tells her daughter a series of stories about
life on Guam before the daughter was born and when she was a baby.
   ISBN 0-395-71548-2
   [1. Guam — Fiction.   2. Mothers and daughters — Fiction.]
I. Tillotson, Katherine, ill.   II. Title.
PZ7.K4575So   1995   94-24581
[Fic] — dc20   CIP
                                                      AC

Printed in the United States of America

HOR   10   9   8   7   6   5   4   3   2   1

CONTENTS

THE DARK, DAMP PLACES OF THE JUNGLE

"Before you were born," Mama begins, "we lived on an island in the middle of the ocean. Blue water washed wood, shells, and coconuts onto the beach. The sand was hot. Palm trees sprouted from the coconuts. The jungle sprouted from the palm trees.

1

"In the middle of the island, the jungle was thick with trees. Vines wrapped around the trunks and stretched from limb to limb. Leaves covered the holes and hollows in the ground.

"The jungle was filled with dark, damp places. In each of these places lived a . . ." Mama smiles at me and says in a deep rumble: "FROG!"

I love frogs.

"Papa and I would walk in the evenings and —"

"Why do they live in the jungle?" I ask. "I always thought frogs lived in ponds."

"Frogs like to live where it's wet. The wettest place on the island is the ocean. But frogs don't like salt water. The *next* wettest places are the waterfalls. But frogs don't like water crashing down on their heads —"

"I don't either," I tell Mama.

She nods. "Then you'd make a good frog. And the *next* wettest places are the dark, damp places of the jungle. So the frogs live there. Anyway, Papa and I would walk in the evenings. The frogs rumbled and grumbled and groaked."

"Was I there?" I ask Mama.

"Sort of. I was pregnant."

2

"Were you really big?"

"No. You were a speck. You were as small as a grain of sand. We didn't even know you were in there. *You were hiding.*"

I don't remember being that small. But I still like to hide. "Tell me more," I say.

"Those were froggy days. We would go to the highest cliffs on the island. The beach stretched far below. The horizon was a blue arc of ocean. During the rainy season, we'd ride our bicycles to the cliffs to watch the big, gray clouds come in.

"After it rained, the whole island smelled wet. Frogs would emerge from the swollen jungle. They'd hop down the road to get where they were going.

"Once we were riding our bicycles to the frog cliffs. It had just rained. The road was wet and sixteen dozen frogs were hopping around. We had to ride carefully. Some of the frogs hopped out of our way. But the biggest frogs just sat there. We had to steer around them.

"We turned onto the last stretch of road. It ran right through the jungle. At the edge of the road were three black shapes, standing still. They were animals, but we

3

couldn't tell what kind. They were big, almost as big as our bicycles."

"What were they?" I ask.

"At first we didn't know. They were too small to be cows and too big to be dogs. They were strong and solid. They didn't move an inch.

"Slowly we pedaled our bicycles. Slowly we rode toward them. Suddenly, the three turned and crashed into the jungle. Mud splattered onto the road. Branches cracked and snapped. As they turned, we saw their tusks: sharp and menacing. We knew then that they were wild boars. They were faster and meaner than any pig in a farmyard pen.

"Now, I was startled, but Papa . . . Was Papa scared?"

I shake my head. Papa's never scared.

"That's right. Your papa popped a wheelie. Then he rode straight into the trees, following the boars. He disappeared into the dark, damp places of the jungle."

"He chased the boars on his bicycle?"

"Yep."

"What did you do?"

"I stood there, amazed. After a while I realized that

my mouth was hanging open, so I closed it," Mama laughs.

"Why were you amazed?" I ask.

"They were completely hidden behind the vines, first the boars and then Papa. It was like the jungle had swallowed them up," Mama shrugs. "They were *gone*."

"Did Papa ever catch up to the boars?"

"Nope," Mama says. "But I learned two things that day that I took with me all the while I was on the island."

"What was the first one?" I ask.

"You can find almost *anything* in the jungle, from frogs to boars to papas riding bicycles."

"What was the other one?"

"Some of the best things on the island are hidden."

FEEDING FISHES

"Tell me another song about the island," I say.

"They're not songs, they're stories."

"I know they're stories. But they seem like songs." I'm not sure how to explain it. Mama sounds different when she talks about the island. Different from when she's telling me to brush my teeth or asking what I want for lunch. She sounds kind of soft and sleepy. She sounds like she's somewhere else, somewhere she likes a lot. "It's the way your voice is when you tell them."

Mama smiles. "Okay. Here's a song about feeding fish.

"Before you were born, you lived on an island in the middle of the ocean. The waters around the island were bright with fish of many colors. There were yellow fish the color of daffodils, and these were yellow tangs. There were blue fish with fat lips, and these were trig-gerfish. There were red-and-white striped fish with sharp quills, and these were lionfish.

"One day Papa and I went snorkeling —"

"Was I there?" I ask.

"Yep. I was in the ocean and you were in my belly."

"Did you know I was in there?"

"I wasn't sure. You were only the size of a pea. I couldn't *feel* you, but I thought you *might* be in there."

"Hah!" I laugh. "Then I was still hiding!"

"It was the first time I had ever snorkeled. We waded out until the water was waist-deep. I pushed my face into the rubbery smell of the mask. I pulled the strap around the back of my head. The mask was so tight that it pinched my cheeks and tugged on my hair."

"Did it hurt?" I ask.

"It was uncomfortable. But if your mask isn't tight then the water leaks in."

"I don't think I'd like it. I don't even like to pull a tight shirt over my head."

"Wait and see," Mama smiles. "I didn't think I'd like it, either. In fact, Papa had to hold my hand. Then I eased myself into the warm blue ocean.

"Now, a strange thing happens the first time you go snorkeling: *You hear yourself breathe*. It seems so loud! Every breath, in and out, in and out, sounds like you're hooked up to a respirator. It sounds as if a machine is breathing for you. And if that sound makes you nervous? Well, then you hear your breathing grow even faster.

"Papa hadn't warned me about that. Maybe he'd been snorkeling so many times he'd forgotten. But that was the first thing I noticed when I put my head underwater. Until I got used to the rhythmic roar of my own breath, I didn't even see all the colors.

"But there they were: blue starfish sucking on the

coral, black sea cucumbers rolling with the waves, lavender sea anemones waving in the currents. With my mask on, I could see all the way to the ocean floor.

"It was my first time snorkeling. Papa wanted to make it special. So he brought along a bag of food to feed the fish. And do you know what he brought?"

I take a wild guess. "Fish food?"

"Peas. Frozen peas. When I saw that bag of frozen peas, I thought your Papa was crazy. But it was true. We pulled peas by the handful out of the bag. The peas floated in the warm water. The fish swam right up in front of us and ate. They were so close that I could stroke them.

"The large fish opened their mouths and took the peas in whole. But for the small fish, even a pea was too big. They would open their mouths as wide as they could. But the peas just bounced off their lips and drifted slowly downward."

"They couldn't even eat one pea?" I ask. "I can fit ten on my fork at one time!"

Mama shakes her head. "Nope. For these small fish, we crushed peas in our hands. The water grew cloudy with mashed pea, and then even the little fish could eat.

"Papa and I fed peas to the fishes, and you were the size of a pea inside me."

CRAB RACES

"A few weeks later, I knew you were in there," Mama smiles.

"How did you know?" I ask.

"Well, for one thing, I started throwing up a lot."

"In the ocean?"

"No!" Mama laughs. "In the bathroom."

"Why'd you throw up?"

"I don't know," she shrugs. "When you're pregnant, you throw up a lot."

"I hate to throw up. I hate it!"

"Me, too," Mama says. "But I got pretty good at it. I threw up all the time. For weeks and weeks."

I didn't know that. It sounds terrible. "Were you mad?" I ask.

"At you? No, I was happy. And scared."

"What were you scared of?"

"I was doing something I'd never done before. I wasn't sure how to do it."

That's how I feel sometimes. "Was Papa scared?"

"Not much," Mama says. "He said that having a baby is like having an adventure."

"Tell me another adventure," I say.

"Before you were born, you lived on an island in the middle of the ocean. This island was ringed with flat, sandy beaches. On each of these beaches lived hermit crabs. Hundreds of hermit crabs, some barely larger than the grains of sand.

"Now, hermit crabs are tricky animals. Find an empty

shell on a sandy shore. Flip it over. It may be just an empty shell. But find that same shell on the same sandy shore. Flip it over. You are just as likely to discover the bony, purple plates of a belly and claw tucked into a tiny shield.

"Papa and I would place bets, guessing which shells held those tiny crabs —"

"What did you get if you won?" I ask.

Mama shakes her head. "Nothing. You didn't get anything."

That seems like a dumb game. "What did you get if you lost?"

"Ah! If you lost, then you had to carry the picnic basket down the beach."

"Did I bet, too?" I ask.

"You weren't born yet. You were still tucked into a tight little bulge in the middle of my belly."

"Your belly *still* wasn't big?"

"No," Mama smiles. "But it was getting bigger.

"Another bet we used to make was whose crab would win the race. Papa would dig a shallow hole in the sand. He'd find *his* champion crab. I'd find *my* champion crab. Both crabs had to be smaller than my thumbnail. Sometimes Papa tried to use a crab that was too big, but I always caught him.

"Papa liked to choose tough crabs with shells like thick armor. He thought they'd be stronger, like little tanks crossing the desert. But I chose smaller crabs with thin shells. I figured they'd be a lot faster.

"Anyway, we'd check the sizes. Then the crab race would begin! We'd put the two champions into the hole and —"

"How big was the hole?" I ask.

"About a foot around."

"How deep was it?"

"A couple inches."

I shake my head. "That's not very deep."

"It is if you're smaller than my thumbnail. Anyway, we'd put the two champions into the hole and see who could scuttle out first.

"Anything was fair as long as we didn't touch the crabs. Papa would get down on his knees, put his ear to the sand, and look his crab straight in the eye. 'Come on, Rocky. Come on, tough guy!' he'd say in a low growl. 'Move it!'

"I'd just cheer, 'Go! Go! Go!' Whenever my crab

stopped, I'd blow a little puff of air on its tail."

"Whose crab won?" I ask.

"Sometimes Papa's, but usually mine. Papa's crabs had such nice, thick shells that they felt safe anywhere. They didn't move unless they wanted to. They were a little stubborn. But my crabs used speed for protection. They were used to moving and they moved all the time. And you know what? Mine were not only faster; they were prettier, too.

"My little purple crabs were smaller than my thumbnail. Their claws were the size of freckles. Their shells were as thin as a sheet of paper. But when we held our crab races, they were champions, just the same."

THE FLUTTER
OF WINGS, THE
CLATTER OF SHELLS

Mama makes some tea. I get some juice. "That was a
racing song," she says. "But this is a quiet song and we
must be quiet to sing it." We tiptoe back to the couch.

"What is this song called?" I whisper.

" 'The Flutter of Wings, The Clatter of Shells,' "

Mama says. "Are you ready to hear them?"

I nod.

"Before you were born, you lived on an island in the middle of the ocean. This island was crawling with crabs, some barely larger than the grains of sand. Not all the crabs were tiny, though, as we discovered the day we hiked to the swimming hole.

"To reach the swimming hole we had to hike a mile down the beach. There weren't many people on this stretch of sand because it headed away from the fancy hotels. The farther we walked, the more the beach looked like it didn't belong to anybody. I almost felt bad that we were leaving footprints behind us. But I knew that the ocean would wash them away."

"Did I leave footprints, too?" I ask. "Little baby foot-prints?"

Mama shakes her head.

"I wasn't born *yet*?" I ask. "I can't believe it's taking so long!"

Mama shrugs. "You'll be born soon. Just a few more songs, I promise. But you know what? In this song my belly is bigger, and you're kicking inside me all the time!"

"Okay," I say.

"So, we walked a mile down the beach, the ocean on our left, a row of palm trees on our right. Clouds of black butterflies hovered beneath the palms. We walked right into the flutter of their wings."

"What did it feel like?" I ask.

"It tickled." Mama blows on my cheek. "Like that. Soon we came to the path that led inland. The sun was hot and bright on the beach, but the jungle smelled like warm, wet earth.

"We followed the twisted path deep into the dark, damp places of the jungle. Papa went first, his rubber thongs slapping the bottoms of his feet.

"Now, I *knew* that the jungle wouldn't be silent. There were too many frogs for that. I *expected* to hear the rustling sound of a thousand frogs moving under wet leaves. I *knew* we'd see them scrambling up vines and hopping down the path on their webbed feet.

"But I *didn't* expect to hear that strange, clattering sound, like pebbles being tossed on a sidewalk. You kicked me once, as if to say, 'Stop!' So I did. Papa walked on ahead but I stopped to listen. The jungle clunked and clanked and clattered.

"It was then that I realized . . ." Mama waits. Her eyes grow narrow. She leans toward me and whispers: *"There was something else moving on the jungle floor!"*

I feel a shiver on the back of my neck. "What was it?"

"I put my hand to my belly. 'What do you think, Spud?' I asked you. We called you Spud because you bulged out like a potato growing in the ground.

" 'What do you think, Spud?' But you only turned over and went to sleep."

"I went to sleep?" I say. "How could I sleep at a time like that?"

Mama shrugs. "I crouched down and looked into the vines and branches. There were brown shapes rustling in the leaves. Brown creatures were creeping around on the ground. They were crawling across the path, right by my feet. Were those *rocks* moving?"

"They were crabs!" I shout.

"Crabs!" Mama says. "Giant brown hermit crabs the size of my fist. They scuttled across the rutted jungle floor, thunking their shells against the rocks. They pulled themselves up, digging their claws in to hold on. If the rock was too steep, they sometimes rolled off altogether. They looked so clumsy that I started laughing.

"I laughed all the way to the swimming hole, a deep pond filled with muddy water. But I had to wait to tell Papa about my discovery. For just as I reached the hole, he swung out over the water, clutching the knot of a rope swing with his strong feet. '*There* you are!' he said. Then he dropped into the water with a huge splash."

SWIFT GRAY SHAPES

"Did you jump into the swimming hole, too?" I ask.

"No. I told Papa I didn't think it was safe because you were in my belly."

"Oh."

"But the real reason I didn't jump in was because I was scared."

"What were you scared of?"

"The water was so brown that I couldn't see into it. I didn't know what else was in there. Almost anything can live in the jungle."

"Papa wasn't scared?" I ask.

"Nope."

"He'd jump into anything," I say. "Papa's never scared."

"Of course he is. Everyone's scared sometimes. I know a song about a time when Papa was scared. Do you want to hear it?"

I have to think about this. I didn't know that Papa *got* scared. "I'm not sure."

"Sit here," Mama says. She pats the cushion right beside her.

Usually I don't do that anymore. I let her rub my back but I don't let her hold me. Unless I'm sick. Or scared. Or I'm going to be scared . . . I scoot up next to Mama. "What is this song called?"

" 'Swift Gray Shapes.' " She pulls me close. "Before you were born, you lived on an island in the middle of the ocean. The sun rose over this island each morning precisely at dawn.

"One cloudy dawn, Papa stood alone on the beach. He wanted to swim early, before the tourists chased away all the big fish. He pulled his long, rubber dive suit over his feet and up his legs. He slid his arms into the sleeves and zipped up the belly. Papa was going scuba diving.

"Scuba diving is even better than snorkeling. You carry air in the tank on your back. You can stay underwater for a long time. You can sneak up on all the fish.

"Papa waded out into the ocean until the water lapped at his chest. Then he sank into the dim, chilly water. Angel fish swam by in black-and-white striped schools. Moorish idols nibbled his neck. Moray eels poked their speckled heads out of the rocks. Then Papa saw a sweet brown face peeking out from beneath a coral head.

"Now, a raccoon pufferfish is about the most timid of all ocean creatures. He's called a raccoon puffer because he looks like a raccoon: all tan with a mask of chocolate brown over his face. He doesn't have sharp teeth and he can't swim very quickly. He tends to hide a lot.

"But he does have a special defense. If he ever feels threatened, he can suck in water like a water balloon. Then he is as big as an eggplant.

"The trouble is, once a raccoon puffer has puffed himself up, he's so heavy with water that he can't move at all. And that's what happened to the sweet brown face that Papa saw. To that little puffer, Papa in his wetsuit was a swift gray shape in the water.

"That poor puffer took one look at Papa and sucked in a pint of water. Then he rested like a small football on the ocean floor.

"Papa didn't want to hurt the puffer, but he was curious: He'd never *held* a fish in the ocean before. He reached down and gently lifted the puffer in his hands. The puffer's skin was soft. Papa cradled him like a puppy. The puffer watched Papa with big, round eyes."

"Was he scared of Papa?" I ask.

"Yes. Papa looked into those big, round eyes and felt bad. So, even though he was curious, he decided to put the puffer back. Crouching down, he gently laid the puffer in the sand. Then Papa froze. For he suddenly noticed swift gray shapes swimming toward him. They were big — as big as Papa — and there were a lot of them."

"What were they?" I ask.

"Papa wasn't sure. They swam right up and skimmed over his head. And as they passed, Papa saw a triangular fin jutting out of each back.

"Now, sharks don't usually swim in groups. They like to be by themselves. The one time you *will* see a lot of sharks together, though, is when there's something good to eat.

"Papa watched with big round eyes as they circled and swam toward him again."

"Did they want to eat Papa?" I ask. My voice sounds squeaky and small.

"Papa didn't want to find out. Remember how I told you that when you're diving, you can hear yourself breathe? And when you get nervous?"

"You hear yourself breathe faster," I say.

Mama nods. "Papa heard himself breathing faster

and faster. He knew he had to stay calm. He felt help-
less, crouched with the pufferfish on the ocean floor.

"The gray shapes approached, heading straight for
Papa. Without thinking, he suddenly stood up. The
shapes turned sharply upward and broke through the
surface of the water. They leaped into the air and dove
back down.

"Papa realized then that they were dolphins. He felt
sad as he watched them swim away. For if he'd known
they were dolphins from the beginning, he would have
tried to swim with them."

"What happened to the puffer?" I ask.

"They were friends after that. Papa learned a lot
about survival from that sweet brown face. Papa
couldn't suck in water like a puffer, but he did the
next best thing to make himself larger."

"He stood up," I say.

"Yep. Papa had always thought that shark teeth and
lionfish quills and stonefish venom were the best ways
to survive in the ocean. On that gray, cloudy dawn,
however, Papa came to appreciate the special defense
of the raccoon puffer: Lie low whenever possible, but if
you need to, make yourself look big."

ONE-EYED CAT

"Let's go back!" I say.

"To the island?" Mama smiles.

"Don't you want to go back? Just to visit?" I ask. "I want to. I don't remember it at all."

"I know," Mama kisses me. "That's why I tell you all

these songs."

"Tell me another one," I say.

"Before you were born," Mama says quietly, "you lived on an island in the middle of the ocean. In the middle of this island was a small house. And on the porch of this house hung a mesh hammock. Papa lay in that hammock every evening."

"The same hammock that we have now?" I ask.

"The same one."

"Did you lie in it, too?"

"No. Papa bought the hammock for me. But by the time he bought it, I was too big. Once I got in, I couldn't get out."

"Did I lie in the hammock?"

Mama shrugs. "You weren't born yet."

What a waste! There we were on that great island, and I didn't get to do anything. No snorkeling, no jungle, no swimming hole, no crab races! "It's not fair! I didn't get to do anything!"

Mama laughs. "Those last few months, I felt exactly the same. I just waited and waited to meet you. I never did swing much in that hammock, but Papa did. He lay in it after work, before dusk brought out the mosquitoes. From the hammock, Papa could peer past the back yard out into the jungle.

"At the jungle's edge there lived a cat, half-wild, with no one to feed it. The cat never let us come near, but that was okay with Papa. I think Papa liked its in-dependence.

"The cat's fur was white with patches of gray and black. It was a tough cat. It only had one good eye but still managed to survive on its own."

"What was its name?" I ask.

"Didn't need one," Mama says. "It was months before we actually saw the cat eat. We figured it must live on frogs. There was no frog shortage in that jungle. Some-times Papa and I would talk about leaving food out for the cat. But it seemed to be doing fine without us.

"Finally, one day Papa saw the cat crouch down, tense and calculating. Suddenly, it leaped into the air. It caught something green in its jaws. Looking for a dry place to eat, the cat slipped up onto the porch.

"Papa lay very still because the cat had never come on the porch before. He watched it eat, not exactly sure what the cat had caught. It didn't look like a frog.

"The cat ate and then washed its face and back. It

closed its eye and slept in the setting sunlight. Finally, Papa rose. The mosquitoes were coming out and they were biting. The cat sprang away as Papa came near."

"What did it eat?" I ask.

"Papa crossed the porch to the spot where the cat had been. He discovered that the cat didn't just live on frogs, it also lived on praying mantises. For all the cat had left behind were two filmy wings.

"We'd see the cat off and on throughout the day, taking a nap or stalking lunch. But Papa liked to watch it best while swinging in the hammock. The hammock creaked softly and rhythmically as the sky darkened. Then the jungle seemed to flatten into a dense wall of shadow and vine.

"Nothing moved in this jungle wall, not even the cat — it *appeared*. It simply *wasn't* and then *was*. And when the cat *was*, it was still. Its patches of gray and black blended into the flat jungle background while the white fur glowed softly.

"It was a twilight stillness that the cat brought to the evenings. Papa watched and wondered about the cat, and it seemed to watch and wonder about Papa. At first Papa thought that he only saw the cat when it wanted to watch him. But finally Papa realized that he only saw the cat when it wanted to be seen."

CEILINGS, WALLS, AND WINDOWS

"Would you like to get born now?"

I sit up. "The song with all the lizards?" I've heard this song before.

Mama nods.

"What are they called, again?"

"Geckoes. On the day you were born, you lived on an island in the middle of the ocean. In the middle of this island was a small house. And on the ceilings, walls, and windows of this house, there lived geckoes.

"Now, geckoes are pretty amazing creatures. They have little pads on their toes. The pads are covered with thousands of tiny hooks, kind of like velcro. Geckoes can walk up walls. They can walk across ceilings. Sometimes I'd look up and there would be a gecko, walking upside down on the ceiling. He'd stop, look around for a while, then walk some more, upside down on the ceiling.

"When you have fifty geckoes living in your house, you get to know them pretty well. I liked them because they ate mosquitoes. They're different colors: gray or brown or green. They have round eyes but they don't have any eyelids. Without eyelids, a gecko can't blink. So it keeps its eyeballs wet with its tiny pink tongue.

"The biggest geckoes are five inches from nostril to tail. They can be pretty territorial. They'll stake out the corner of a window and fight to defend it. Sometimes I'd hear this rattling sound. I'd know that two geckoes were arguing over the same spot in the house. Then I'd find one gecko with its mouth wrapped around the other gecko's head.

"The pregnant geckoes have huge bellies, with an egg on the right and an egg on the left. If I came home at night and the lights were already on, I'd check the windows before I went in. With the light shining behind them, the geckoes became transparent. I could see their insides. There would be two white ovals nestled beneath the spine.

"I was very careful around the pregnant geckoes. I'd see them on the walls and windows, but not on the ceiling. I thought that maybe they were being cautious while they were pregnant. I knew exactly how they felt.

"Once I opened the curtains and found two tiny eggs on the windowsill. I left the eggs alone, and one day they were gone. Two more babies were walking the walls.

"The baby geckoes were my favorites. They were an inch from tip to tail. Can you imagine how small *their* toes were?"

I shake my head and smile. Mama loves babies.

"Those toes were so small that I couldn't even see them. But I knew those tiny toes were covered with thousands of hooks because I'd see baby geckoes walk across the ceiling, stop and look around, and then walk some more.

"There weren't any geckoes in the hospital. It was air conditioned and the windows were sealed. I didn't even notice at first. But later, after Papa had gone home to get some rest, I lay for many hours in that hospital bed, holding you. I wished then that we had something else, quiet and small, to keep us company.

"When we got home, the geckoes were like old friends. I would hold you while you nursed and dozed and then nursed again. Papa was at work, so it was just you and me and the geckoes.

"Those were long, still afternoons. I'd get a tall glass of ice water and set it on the table. You'd nurse and we'd both get sleepy. The icy glass would sweat condensation. When I got too hot, I'd lift the glass to my forehead. It was cold and wet against my skin. All we could hear was the whir of the fan, the clink of ice cubes, and the geckoes rattling on the walls.

"Once, I saw a little head peeking over the table edge. A baby gecko was surveying the landscape. Slowly it reached one and then the other foot onto the table top. It pulled itself up. Then it walked. Over the magazines. Under a tissue. Around the lamp. Through the afternoon, it explored the whole table.

"Finally, it reached the spot where my icy drink had been. A ring of condensation lay on the table top. The tiny gecko drank like a wildebeest at a watering hole. In the sleepy days that followed, I would set my drink out early. And as you nursed and dozed, the tiny gecko would drink deeply from that ring of water.

"I saw other geckoes, of course, but that little one was my favorite because it reminded me of you."

"Of me?" I ask.

"Yep. That little gecko reminded me of you, or of who I hoped you'd be: someone who explored the universe, right-side up and upside down, but stopped every once in a while for a nice, cool drink of water."

FORTY LIVES OR MORE

I look at Mama. "That's it?"

"Yep."

"I got born and that was it?"

"Sorry," she shrugs. "Babies don't do a whole lot at first. You slept and nursed and cried and looked around. And then, when you were a year and a half, we left."

"But didn't *I* get to do anything on the island?"

"You played in the sand."

"That's *all?*" I can't believe it! What about the bicycles and the wild boars? What about the pufferfish and the dolphins? What about walking through butterflies? What about the frozen peas? "That's not fair!"

"Let me think," Mama says. "Well, there *was* the time you helped save forty lives or more." She gets up and starts walking toward the kitchen. "But you're probably not interested in —"

"I am!"

Mama turns around. "Oh! Okay." She sits back down on the couch. "When you were a baby, you lived on an island in the middle of the ocean. It was an island of dolphins and fish, crabs and butterflies, geckoes and boars. But it was also an island of people.

"Every afternoon, as Papa lay in the hammock, I took a walk in the setting sunlight. Women took laundry off the clotheslines. Dogs chased chickens in the yards. Children rode past me on bicycles."

"Did I ride my bicycle, too?" I ask. Then I remember. "Oh, yeah. I was a *baby*. I didn't do *anything*."

"Just wait." Mama smiles. "The people on this island had schools, houses, and stores. And swimming pools.

Deep, blue pools. Cool, shimmering pools. Pools for belly flops.

"Construction workers had cleared a patch of jungle down the road from our house. They were building a swimming pool on our side of the island. Every day I walked past the pool. Sometimes I'd stop and take a look.

"The backhoe dug a pit. The men smoothed the bottom. They poured the foundation. They built the walls. They set the tiles. They leveled the ground for the walkways and patio.

"The men didn't work every day, though. If it rained, they had to wait until the ground dried out. Slowly the sun baked the steaming earth into a hard, flat surface. But the pool just filled with rainwater, inch by inch. Mud from heavy work boots turned this rainwater brown. Leaves from the jungle blew in. Scraps of lumber floated. Pretty soon the shiny new pool looked more like that swimming hole in the jungle: deep, brown, alive."

"What was living in there?" I ask.

"A deep pool of water on the jungle's edge?" Mama says. "Take a guess."

Not fish. Not boars. Not geckoes. And then I know:

"FROGS!"

"That's right," Mama nods. "First one and then forty frogs found this pool of muddy water. They did the breaststroke. They did the backstroke. They bobbed and dove. They stepped on each other's heads to climb onto floating wood.

"They were plump and slimy. They were wet and warty. They ate bugs. They plopped into the water. They filled their throats with moist jungle air. They rumbled and grumbled and groaked.

"One day I stopped to watch the frogs. The construction workers had poured the walkways and the patio. The concrete was already dry, so I knew that the pool was almost done. I figured the frogs would swim one more night. Then in the morning they would hop back into the jungle.

"I walked to the edge of the pool and looked in. The frogs were there, all right. *But the water wasn't.*"

"What do you mean?" I ask.

"The pool had been drained. It was going to be cleaned."

"What about the frogs?"

Mama sighs. "They didn't look so good. The mud on the sides of the pool had already dried. There was a layer of mud on the pool floor. It was still wet but it was getting thick.

"The frogs were hopping around. Sometimes one would try to hop out of the pool. But the sides were too high and the tile was too slick. The frogs didn't look so wet and slimy anymore. They looked dirty and dried out. They looked like they were dying."

"We gotta do something!" I say. I feel my heart start pounding.

Mama nods. "That's just what I thought. I ran all the way home. I crashed into the back yard. Papa sat up in the hammock. The one-eyed cat leaped back into the jungle.

" 'What's wrong?' Papa said. 'What's happened?'

" 'They need our help,' I gasped. 'At the pool.'

"Papa raced inside and lifted you out of your crib. You were still asleep but you woke up, bouncing against Papa's shoulder as he followed me.

" 'Has someone drowned?' he asked. 'A child?'

" 'They're all dying!' I started to cry.

" 'Here! Take the baby!' Papa shouted. He handed you to me and then sprinted ahead."

GOOEY, GLUEY MUD

"It took me a few minutes to reach the pool," Mama continues. "I was out of breath and you were heavy. When I got there, Papa was sitting on the edge, his feet dangling into empty space. He was laughing.

" 'Oh, honey,' he said to me, panting and laughing at the same time. 'I thought someone was dying.'

" 'Someone *is*,' I said. 'Look at them. They're all dying.'

" 'They're *frogs*,' he said.

" 'They're *dying* frogs.' "

"Papa didn't want to help?" I ask.

" 'Honey, there are a million frogs on this island,' he told me.

" 'One million and *forty*,' I said."

"Papa didn't want to help?" I ask again. "I can't believe it."

"Well," Mama says, "in a way he was right. There were lots of frogs on the island. But these frogs were here, right in front of us. I knew we had to try. 'When I climb into bed and close my eyes tonight,' I told Papa, 'I'm going to see these frogs. And you will, too. How would you rather picture them? Swinging on vines in the jungle, or slowly baking on the bottom of the pool?' "

I nod. "You got him."

Mama smiles. "Yep. I got him. Papa sighed and hopped into the pool. He grimaced as his feet hit the bottom. The gooey mud oozed between his toes. He reached down and plucked a frog like it was a nice fat grape. 'See? Easy,' he said. Then the frog wriggled out of his grasp and plopped back into the mud.

" 'Come on in,' Papa smiled to me. 'The water's fine!' "

"You went in, too?" I ask. That doesn't sound like Mama. She gets dirty sometimes but she never gets slimy.

"I sat down and took off my shoes. I put you next to them. 'Stay away from the pool, Spud,' I told you. We still called you Spud because you were so small. 'Stay by Mama's shoes.' So you sat and chewed on the laces, and I climbed into the pool.

"As soon as my feet touched the bottom, I shuddered. The mud was gross. It was sticky and slick at the same time. It felt like glue. Or Jello. And it smelled terrible: fishy, moldy, rotten.

"At first we tried to pick the frogs up, one by one. But they were too quick and slippery for that. Soon our hands and arms were covered with goo. I caught one frog. It scrambled up my arm. I felt its gluey webbed feet on the back of my neck. It pushed off and leaped into the mud.

"A mosquito landed on my cheek and I slapped it without thinking. Then I had mud on my face, too.

"We found that the best way to catch the frogs was to

herd them like sheep. As soon as we came near, they hopped away from us. So we chased them into a corner of the pool. Then we scooped them out, using our hands like shovels.

"Once they were out of the pool, the frogs hopped once or twice. Then they sat, watching us.

"We were doing pretty well. I counted seven or eight frogs outside the pool. They just sat there. Sometimes one would hop a few times in no particular direction. But we were making progress. I started to feel pretty good.

"And then a terrible thing happened: The frogs *outside* the pool started to jump back *in*. My heart sank. I stood in the stinking mud and watched the frogs hop back into the pool."

"That's crazy!" I say. "Why would they hop back in? Didn't they realize they were going to die?"

"I don't know." Mama shakes her head. "It seemed crazy to me, too. But after all those weeks of swimming, the frogs must have felt the pool was home.

" 'That's it, honey,' Papa said quietly. 'We tried. Let's go home.'

" 'No!' I cried. I was frustrated but I was mad, too. Mad at the frogs who wouldn't even try to save themselves. I scooped up three frogs and stuck them on the walk. 'GET OUT OF HERE, YOU STUPID FROGS!'

"When I started yelling, you put down my shoe and toddled over. You'd only been walking a few months, but you were getting pretty good at it. As you reached the pool, the biggest frog hopped away. You followed it. In a minute, it disappeared into the jungle.

" 'That's it!' I said. 'Spud can chase them away. Get the frog, sweetie!' I said to you. 'GET THE FROG!'

"You laughed and ran after another frog. When it hopped into the jungle, you almost started to cry. 'No, no, sweetie,' I said. 'Here's another one! Get *this* frog!'

"Pretty soon you were running back and forth in front of the pool, shrieking and laughing. Papa and I scooped out the frogs and you chased them into the jungle. 'It's working!' I shouted. I felt so happy! I felt like hopping around in the mud with the other frogs!"

"I saved the frogs?" I ask.

"Yep," Mama smiles. "You chased them into the jungle. We would have given up if it hadn't been for you. We couldn't have saved them if you hadn't chased them to safety."

So I *did* do something! Even though I was a baby! I saved forty frogs in one afternoon!

THE LAST FROG

"So I saved all the frogs!" I say.

"Almost," Mama smiles. "Almost all the frogs.

"We'd been slipping, sliding, and scooping for more than an hour. You had personally saved frog after frog. We'd almost cleared the pool," Mama says. "All except for one. The other frogs had let us chase them into the corners and scoop them out. But *this* frog was different: He was huge. He was stubborn. *He was a blob frog*."

"A what?" I ask.

"A blob frog," Mama says. "He had a green blob head and brown blob legs. His spotted belly flattened into a puddle of frog when he sat down. He wallowed in himself, his tiny yellow arms resting on his belly blubber."

"Euuwww!!" I say.

"He was gross," Mama agrees. "He was wonderful! He just sat there when we came near. He wasn't scared like the other frogs. We couldn't chase him into the corner. And we couldn't catch him, either. Just as our fingertips touched his blob body, he'd leap like a rocket, firing into space. Every time his belly landed, mud splattered our legs.

"I almost felt like I'd met this frog before. He was the kind of frog who would sit right down in the middle of the road after it rained. The kind of frog who wouldn't move over for anyone. The kind of frog who expected all the cars to go around *him*.

"We tried and tried to get that frog out of the pool. We chased him. We yelled at him. We snuck up on him. Papa lunged at him and slipped, landing on his side. Pretty soon we were as muddy as that frog.

"It seemed like we'd never catch him. I was a little afraid that Papa would give up. His leg was bleeding from when he'd slipped. But I shouldn't have worried. The last thing your Papa wanted to admit was that a frog had beaten him. 'You rascal!' Papa said to the frog. He charged and landed on the seat of his pants. He got a gooey grip on the frog's leg, but the frog slipped away. 'You rascal!' Papa said again.

"The frog hopped to the other end of the pool. He turned to face us. He filled his throat with moist jungle air. And then we heard a roaring sound like a herd of buffalo sweeping the plain. The blob frog rumbled, grumbled, and GROAKED!"

" 'Enough!' Papa said in disgust. 'Save yourself.' He climbed wearily out of the pool."

"Papa was mad at the frog?" I ask.

"When we started chasing the blob frog, we thought that he was scared of us. But the big 'groak' changed all that. We realized that the frog wasn't scared of anything. The frog was teasing us. The frog was laughing at us. Nobody likes to be laughed at, especially by a frog.

'Save yourself,' Papa said. He picked you up in his muddy arms. 'Let's go home,' he told me.

"Suddenly I felt exhausted. I couldn't have chased that frog even if I'd wanted to. I was a little afraid that Papa would have to rescue *me*. But I pulled my aching body out of the pool. 'Sorry,' I said to the blob.

"Even though we'd saved forty frogs, I felt sad. It didn't seem right. Such a magnificent frog shouldn't die, trapped on the bottom of the pool. But we couldn't do any more. I grabbed my shoes and followed Papa.

"Mosquitoes buzzed and bit. I knew that those forty frogs were already feasting on bugs in the jungle. I knew that we'd see those same frogs the next time it rained. They'd be hopping down the road to get where they were going.

"The setting sun had turned the sky rosy. It was a peaceful sky but a sad sky all the same. It was the blob frog's last sunset. I hoped he'd enjoy it.

"We crossed the patio and were almost to the road when we heard it: a low rumble that grew and grew into a *roar!* 'The blob frog!' I cried. I ran back toward the pool, Papa following me.

"Just as we reached the edge, the frog pushed off of

his huge legs. He shot into the air like a rocket. He landed on the walkway.

" 'You rascal,' Papa said. 'You could have saved yourself all the time!'

" '*Urp*,' the frog answered. Then the blob frog hopped into the dark, damp places of the jungle."

"How did Papa feel?" I ask Mama. "Was he mad or happy?"

The door opens. His deep voice calls my name.

"Papa's home," Mama smiles. "Let's find out."